KUCHELA.AI

Sagar Anisingaraju
Prasad Chaganti

KUCHELA.AI

1st Edition: July 2020

Authors
Sagar Anisingaraju
Prasad Chaganti

Design and Illustrations by
Prarthana Siddarth

ISBN: 978-1-64999-843-9

Website: https://www.kuchela.ai

Chapter 1 KUCHELA.AI
San Francisco, USA- January 2020

Exploring humane possibilities, friendship, and values in technology made me embark upon this journey. I have been unable to focus on any other work for the last few days. KUCHELA.AI is the name I gave to the new artificial intelligence project that I started when I began searching for my purpose in life.

Since the day I started planning this project, my mind has been busy with random thoughts. It is going astray. I haven't felt this uneasy, this acute feeling of emptiness since I immigrated to the United States twenty-five years ago. What is happening to me? The cross-functional dream team that I wanted is ready.

The project kick-off meeting was scheduled to start at 10 a.m., but it is 10:15, and I'm still sitting in my office, thinking.

Assuming I'm busy with some in-depth conceptual planning, my executive assistant, Erlyn, has hesitated to disturb me. But with the team waiting in the conference room, she knocks softly on my glass door, calling out, "Krish. Krish!" She points at her watch.

I get up and hurriedly walk to the conference room.

Sorry, I have not introduced myself yet. My name is Krishna Bhamidipati. People call me Krish, and back home in India, they used to call me Krishna.

Till recently, I used to be at Google, heading one of its Advanced AI Research Labs, with a staff of over a hundred people. I left Google and founded my current company called KUCHELA.AI, and hired a small team. My team is highly talented, mostly graduates of MIT, Berkeley, Stanford, IIT, Harvard, and other Ivy League schools.

My fifty-plus patents and over two hundred research papers combined pale in comparison with the collective intellectual output of my team. All are experts in AI technologies, psychology, and economics. Even though they have no clue about the details of KUCHELA.AI, out of deep respect for my research work, my reputation, and the worldwide reach of my prior products, they left their previous jobs and joined my startup. It's time for me to reveal why I assembled them.

"Team, I don't believe in small talk, and so will come directly to the point. Our new project is called KUCHELA.AI. The long-term vision of the project is …"

Suddenly, my mind is going somewhere else, as if in a trance. Why am I becoming distracted?

"Krish, are you okay?" Melinda asks. "We've been waiting to hear from you," says Stella.

I do not respond.

Chapter 2 Saradhi
Amalapuram, India- 1970

Humanity's quest for knowledge started with inquisitiveness. Questioning everything around us, with an innate urge to identify new ways of doing our tasks, has led to advances in science, technology, and knowledge, and the comforts that we enjoy today.

It is, however, debatable if the real benefits of science have reached one and all across the globe uniformly. Economic inequality, healthcare, food, and water shortages in several countries tell us that progress toward an acceptable standard quality of life is still unreachable for certain parts of our global society. However, time does not always move at the same pace. The rate of change in the quality of life has been rapidly increasing in recent times. Let us see its impact through the lens of current happenings around us.

The sun is slowly emerging in the eastern skies, and stars are fading away. Sunshine is slowly battling the darkness and making its impact.

My Tatha (Grandpa), got up with the sound of his alarm and immediately started waking me up from my deep sleep.

"Krishna, wake up. Time to take out the book."

"Tatha, please, let me sleep for ten more minutes," I groaned, and pulled the bedsheet over my head.

"If you get up quickly and study for an hour, I will take you to the river and teach you how to walk on water."

That was enough of an incentive for me. Walk on water? I was unable even to swim, and I had some scores to settle on that front. I got up quickly, got ready, and made a show of completing my studies. My mind was already at the riverfront.

"Krishna, drink your Ovaltine and then go," said my mom, who was always after my food intake. Other than ensuring my food consumption, I doubted if she had anything else in life.

I hurriedly gulped the Ovaltine and rushed out. Tatha was already waiting outside with his bike. I could not control my laughter at seeing him there on the bike. He'd forgotten to tie his pajamas, and the strings were hanging down on both sides.

"Oh, idiot, thanks for pointing that out. Let's go, and we will spend about an hour swimming, and then I have to drop you back to school."

He left me at the banks, did some Surya Namaskaras, and poured some water into the river with folded hands, offering it to the rising sun.

"Tatha, do you think that the Sun God will take the water you are offering?"

"Krishna, answer my questions first. Do humans need sunlight?"

"Of course, Tatha, what kind of question is that?"

"What about rains?"

"Yes."

"And shade?"

"Yes—we need water, sun, and shade."

"Your science teacher must have told you how plants make carbohydrates from sunlight. What do we do when guests come to our house first? We offer water. Similarly, we treat the Sun God, who is giving food to all living beings, as our guest. When he rises daily in the morning, we offer water out of respect. You can also call that respect or *Bhakti*."

9

So I took some water and poured it into the river with my small hands, just as Tatha had done.

"Tatha, I need to learn to swim and want to be faster than my friend Saradhi. He can even swim underwater now!"

"Krishna, I will happily teach you to swim. You will swim as fast as Saradhi very soon."

"By the way, I like your friend, Saradhi. He is a boy with a good heart. Do you know the meaning of his name? Saradhi means the one who guides and gives direction. In the great Mahabharat epic, Lord Krishna was the *saradhi* for the people who were fighting for justice. I want both of you to be good friends, supporting and guiding each other," said Tatha.

I think he realized the tone of jealousy I had when referring to Saradhi's swimming prowess. I was glad he also liked my best friend. But even with friends, you needed to be on equal footing on some skills, and I was determined to improve my swimming.

Tatha supported my back and helped me float in the water. Slowly, I began to get a grip on the backstroke.

Chapter 3 Friendship Is life
India 1976

<u>High School, Amalapuram</u>

It was the last day of the tenth-grade final exams. I ran out after the bell into the corridors. Saradhi was already waiting there for me.

"Hai Krishna, how was the test? I answered 100 percent of the questions."

"Same for me, Saradhi—the test was easy-peasy compared to what I expected."

"Our preparation certainly helped. What are your plans for the holidays?"

"My Tatha is taking me to Vizag city. We are planning to see the beach, shipyard, and nearby parks there. What about you?"

"You were born with a silver spoon in your mouth, Krishna. I am not that lucky. I need to teach kids in my village and earn some money. Dad is not in good health, so I am not in the mood to go out anywhere during the holiday."

I felt sad for Saradhi and told him that I would just make a short trip and come back as soon as possible. We shook hands and left. I knew I would probably see him in junior college soon.

Konaseema Bhanoji College, Amalapuram

My heart was filled with a sense of happiness when I first entered junior college. I parked my bike in the stands and went into my classroom. Saradhi and I both joined the group called MPC, where Math, Physics, and Chemistry were the major subjects. We sat together in our class. We'd joined a prestigious college. Great people had graduated from here, and the college had a reputation for some outstanding teachers.

Introductions to other students were taken care of on the first day. Principal Mr. Sanuel lectured us about the prestige and discipline of the school during our first class. He gave us stencil copies of English-to-Telugu translations for some technical English words. For most of us who'd studied in our vernacular Telugu until now, reading science and other subjects in English was quite the ordeal.

There were no lessons on the first day before lunch. During the lunch break, Saradhi and I opened our tiffin boxes. We were eagerly talking about the college and the science labs that

12

we were going to see the next day. Instead of waiting till the next day, we finished our lunch sooner and peeked into the Physics labs.

Mr. Seshagiri Rao, head of the Physics Department, saw us and invited us inside. After realizing that we were the new MPC students, he took us around and explained the lab. It was quite big, with several types of equipment.

In his monotone voice, he told us, "Listen, I do not like anyone coming late to my classes or being absent. The same rules apply to you as well. Be prompt with your studies, and learn."

We obediently nodded our heads and came out. We were impressed with his stature and the way he explained the fundamentals of physics in both theory and practical classes. After Tatha's homeschooling and inspiration around math, Mr. Seshagiri gave me a foundation and interest in physics.

As we grew into young adulthood, we started forming our own opinions about life. Interest in the subjects and education kept both Saradhi and me at the top of our class. We both wanted to learn more and agreed that we should pursue Engineering degrees.

However, life is not always fair, especially if you are not among the economically privileged class. Saradhi had significant disturbances in his family life around that time. His dad passed away suddenly due to a lack of proper medical treatment. They could not afford the care he needed. Losing the only wage-earner in the family burdened Saradhi with extra responsibility. I did my best to support him at that time with class notes, and somehow, he managed to complete his exams.

However, we both knew that Saradhi pursuing higher education in Engineering was going to be a distant dream.

The summer holidays in my hometown were a drag. Saradhi was busy on the home front, and the beauty of coconut trees and greenery was no longer giving me pleasure. One day, Tatha and my parents came into my room.

"Krishna, pack your bags. We are going to the Guntur city tomorrow. I am going to admit you into the Engineering Coaching Center at Ravi College there. I want you to become a great engineer so that I can proudly tell my friends that my grandson is a world-famous engineer one day."

Even my dad and mom reminded me that there had been no engineers in our family until now. I had no hesitation about pursuing their plans.

"Yes, Tatha, my ambition is the same. I promise that I will do my best, but—." As I hesitated, Tatha realized that I had some other nagging doubts and encouraged me to speak up.

"Krishna, what is bothering you? Are you not excited to go to Guntur for coaching?"

"Tatha, of course, I am excited. It is just that my friend, Saradhi, will not be able to afford to come with me to join the coaching classes, and that's disturbing me. Can we take care of him as well?"

"I am happy that you are thinking of helping your friend. Remember the story of Kuchela and Lord Krishna that I once told you about? Both of them were good friends since their school days. Krishna grew up joyful and prosperous. Kuchela, unfortunately, ended up poor, unable even to support his family. But eventually, their paths crossed again, and Krishna helped Kuchela with his needs. When the day comes, remember this story and always extend your helping hand to the needful. However, for that to happen, you first need to create your own identity and stature."

I realized that Tatha had a point and accepted the reality of future college life without Saradhi.

<u>Ravi College, Guntur:</u>
I started wearing full pants around that time. Bellbottom pants, big-collared plaid shirts, and a small mustache was my usual attire those days. With deep respect and humility, I silently entered into Principal CVN Dhan's office. He immediately smiled at me. I guess he liked my humility. People would also tell me that they liked my sharp nose and deep-set eyes.

Principal Dhan immediately gave a verbal entrance test to get a sense of me. I quickly answered all of the questions. He told me that he had given me a higher-standard test than most, and

15

was happy that I was able to complete it. He took me to the Engineering Coaching class.

All the coaching class teachers were excellent. The foundation laid by my Tatha in math, by Mr. Seshagiri Rao in quantum physics, and by Mr. MSN Murthy in calculus helped me very well in the coaching classes. Discipline and rigor were the emphases at the coaching center. We had to get up every day at 4 a.m. and follow a rigorous schedule of study, exercise, and diet until 9 p.m.

I badly missed Saradhi during that period. I started to understand the economic inequalities of life. Though I wasn't sure how much the coaching center would charge, I knew that it was not something that Saradhi could afford. He told me that he had to take care of his small farm and arrange for his sister's marriage. Instead of his engineering dream, he decided to join a local college to complete his degree in economics. Because of this, the world probably lost out on a brilliant engineer. Soon after, All-India entrance results for admission into IITs, better known as JEE, came out.

As expected, I got a single-digit rank and ended up in the ninth spot in the country. We had a small celebration in our town. It felt like the whole town came to congratulate me, my Tatha, and my parents. I had already gotten an admission letter into the Electronics department at IIT Kanpur. My dream was coming true.

"You are becoming an adult now, Krishna, and set to fulfill my ambitions." When Tatha kissed me on my cheeks, I could feel his beard tickling me.

"Even your young mustache is tickling me, Krishna," he said mischievously. He continued, "After you complete engineering, I want you to go to America for higher studies. You should achieve the highest levels there. The world should benefit from your education. More importantly, our country and its underprivileged people should directly get value from your knowledge. Do you get it?" he asked.

"Sure, Tatha, I understand. But is it not an expensive undertaking? Can we afford my education in the USA?"

Tatha assured me that I only needed to focus on my studies, and the family would take care of the rest. I was so fortunate to have such a loving and supporting family.

<u>Indian Institute of Technology, Kanpur:</u>

I fell in love with Kanpur when I went along with my dad to be admitted to the IIT. It was a long, twenty-hour train journey, but I was full of excitement and hardly slept on the train.

Once known as the Manchester of India, Kanpur, on the banks of the Ganges, was a busy city in the northern part of India. It was more famous for its leather and industrial goods than the IIT at that time. The IIT campus is about fifteen kilometers

17

away from the train station, in a small suburb called Kalyanpur. We took a shared auto ride, locally known as Tuk-Tuk, to reach there.

The fact that I was going to spend my next four years on this campus thrilled me. The sprawling buildings and the lawns were impeccable and manicured. I had never seen anything like them in my home town. Dad lectured me about all the usual precautions that fathers give to their young adults.

"Krishna, be careful and aware of your circumstances. Don't talk too much with strangers. Don't think that you are smarter than others. You should learn new things from everyone that you interact with. Your age now is like a fire pit. It looks attractive but can burn you if you can't handle it properly. This college period is the time for you to build your character. Be obedient and nice, but at the same time, be firm, with a clear point of view on things around you. Make new friends. They will be your future support system. Assess them and continue your relationships. More importantly, keep writing letters at least once a week."

My eyes teared up when Dad was leaving me. I was going to be all on my own for the next several years. I'd never been away from home like this before.

On the first day of college, I met a smart guy in the Engineering College Library. He looked extremely sharp, friendly, and witty, and reminded me of a film star from old Telugu movies. I learned that his name was Kumar. He was the one who'd gotten the #1 rank in the JEE exams. I realized that he would be the real competition for me.

With theory classes, labs, and exams, I became quite busy. As expected, I was, of course, in a constant race with Kumar on all the tests.

When first-semester results came out, Kumar got the highest marks, and I came in second. It gave me more focus to concentrate and study. Kumar's friendship also forced me to learn more about American universities, schools, and programs. The ambition to go there and pursue higher studies took deep roots. I became quite busy with my classwork. Gradually, the letter-writing to home, the occasional communication with Saradhi—it all started fading away.

Professor Sanyal taught us Automata Theory, and Professor Kameswara Rao taught Advanced Communications. Kumar and I became the most coveted students for both these teachers. I got a severe viral fever during the second year, during which time I could not even go out of the hostel. Roommates brought me medicine from the clinic. As I was not attending the classes, Professor Kameswara Rao inquired after me, and one day ended up visiting me at my hostel room along with a doctor. That was an honor that I could never forget.

Once I recovered and went back, he repeated the classes that I'd missed, giving some vague excuses for doing so. My classmates realized that he was doing it out of favoritism to me and were quite jealous. The real bonding between a good

19

student and a teacher has no boundaries. Students were usually scared even to raise their voices against Professor Kameswara Rao. But, based on that incident, they realized how soft his inner self was. Even our Dean was surprised at this gesture by Professor Rao.

I remember one other event vividly. Dr. Sanyal would often set very high standards for his exam. We were all sitting at multiple levels on the benches in L5 Lecture Hall to take his final exam. Kumar and I were in the first row, near the ground level. Dr. Sanyal gave us the question papers first and then went up the steps to distribute the same to the rest of the fifty-plus-student class. It took him about twenty minutes to come back down. As he returned, we both turned in our answer sheets. Dr. Sanyal smiled and said, "I will not be surprised if all of you turn in blank papers. I have made the test very hard."

Kumar and I simultaneously answered, "No, sir, we answered 100 percent of the questions and are done with our exam."

I can't forget the admiration of Dr. Sanyal and the spark he had in his eyes, seeing two of his favorite students exceeding his expectations.

Kumar and I were neck-and-neck during those four years. There was no question of anyone else taking the top two ranks in the class. In the final year, we took the GRE and TOEFL exams to gain admission into MS programs. It was only a matter of time until some acceptance letters arrived.

After the final exams, I bid goodbye to my beloved professors, my college friends, and the city of Kanpur. With a heavy heart, I went to my hometown, Amalapuram. I knew that a new chapter would soon be written in my journey.

Chapter 4 Saradhi vs. Krishna
Amalapuram, India- 1983

For the first time, I got bored with my hometown. Tatha was not his usual self. Age was showing upon him, and he was mostly resting. Father, as always, was busy with his work. Mom was just occupied with cooking and stuffing me with my favorite dishes. We hardly had anything in common to talk about or share.

I suddenly remembered my childhood friend Saradhi. It had been ages since I'd talked with him. The previous year, when he'd come to Kanpur for some student federation meeting, he'd mentioned that he would be pursuing a B.Ed. after graduation to get teaching credentials. It looked like he wanted to settle in our hometown and teach kids. Thinking of him, I went to his house.

As soon as he saw me, Saradhi's face lit up. He dismissed the students he was coaching and then took me aside with a hug. I briefly chatted with his sister and his aging mother. After a small chai and snacks, we both went out on a stroll to our favorite place, the banks of the river. Both of us had spent countless days on those banks together, swimming, talking, flying kites, and playing.

It was fun to watch small kids swimming there while we were sitting. I remembered that it was the envy of Saradhi being a better swimmer that had led me to learn to swim. Overtaking Saradhi in swimming used to be my sole ambition in those days.

"Come out of your thoughts, Krishna. How are you doing? How was college all these four years?"

"First, tell me about yourself, Saradhi. What are your plans moving forward?"

"Oh, my plans are quite simple. After getting my teaching credentials with the B.Ed., I will become a school teacher. Meanwhile, I am already teaching poor students in the evenings. The rest of my free time all goes to several welfare programs I run."

"What welfare programs? What do you mean?"

"I lead a few social programs here. The goal is to educate the underprivileged about their rights, get them excited, and coach

23

them to question authority if they get cheated. Most of the people here are still living in abject poverty, even after many years of independence. Access to basic education and healthcare is still a myth for them. As you know, even my dad passed away without proper medical care."

I'd never seen this side of Saradhi; he had such intensity. I, however, felt that he was misdirected. "Saradhi, what can you do? There are people in positions of higher authority to tackle those problems."

"No Krishna, the system needs a total overhaul. The middlemen and red tape are crushing society. Very little from the government programs, if any, is reaching the needy. The poor are looking for someone to lead and help. I feel that I should be one to lead without waiting for someone else."

"What can you do alone, Saradhi? Let the government officials do that work. Why do you have to waste your brilliance?"

"No, the government will not listen unless we lead the masses to question them. Who else is there to support them otherwise? These underprivileged are my calling, Krishna. My roots are here."

I did not want to argue with him. I did not have the proper viewpoint to convince him, even though I did not like his line of thinking. I was getting a bit tired of the discussion. If he had not been my childhood best friend, I would have left. I was now fully occupied with my admissions and plans in the USA.

My mind was tilted toward the Western ways and against the social leanings and thinking of people like Saradhi.

"Let us discuss your plans, Krishna. What are you going to do now?"

"Well, I already applied to a bunch of schools in the USA. I am expecting to get admitted in a few places. After my MS, I will do my research there." An element of confidence and arrogance sounded in my response to him.

"Oh, so you are going to be a servant of the Americans then?" I could sense the negative tone in his question.

"What do you mean, servant? They will give me admission only if they see merit in me. It is a competitive environment on an international level. Don't we all need to grow? Life is not static. It should be continuously evolving."

"I will not argue on that point, Krishna. Just make sure that you use your intelligence to uplift the world instead of contributing to its destruction. The world, this country, and this town need your future services. Goodbye, and good luck."

I could see that our paths had moved in entirely different directions now. Saradhi was now just a childhood memory for me. He was living in the past. I needed to look forward. These were my thoughts while heading home.

Chapter 5 Stepping Stones for Growth

How do we achieve satisfaction? With money, power, influence, or something else? This is probably a hard question to answer. It all depends on a person's relative viewpoint at any given time.

Internally, Saradhi's perspective was in a state of flux. Right from childhood, he was a deep thinker. For him, the purpose of education was only to uplift society's more vulnerable people.

After parting ways with Krishna due to philosophical differences, he continued reading in libraries and online during his spare time. He spent most of his time learning about socialists and those who worked selflessly for the masses. Such reading had a significant influence on him.

His beliefs firmed up his personal definition of growth. In his view, growth was not when you earned millions of rupees, but when you won the love of millions of people. History books always had a chapter or two for those who made selfless contributions to humanity. We will see many more new chapters written in the years to come.

Saradhi's quest for knowledge, however, did not stop. He kept himself abreast of the changing technology landscape and its influence on humans, globalization, and other developments. He was continually looking for ways to make those advances reach the poorest of the poor. While working as a teacher in our small town, he reached out to several like-minded people over the internet and traveled across India extensively. For several of his social programs, he reached out to government officials and politicians. However, he could not accept the payments that he had to give to various lobbyists and the red tape that was inherent in the system, so he chose to move forward without them.

Instead of relying on these government funds, he started using personal money and time to implement his welfare ideas on a limited scale.

Across the world, thousands of such Saradhis are continually striving to ensure that the value of progress reaches the downtrodden. Such social reformers are the stepping stones for the growth of society. However, to scale those noble tasks and programs, is money alone enough? What if the current generation of technology could be added to them to propel the value proposition globally?

Chapter 6 First Steps in America
Berkeley, USA- 1983

As soon as I completed my engineering degree with Honors at IIT Kanpur, I got accepted into the University of California, Berkeley, with a scholarship, for two years of a Master's Program, and three years of an integrated PH.D. Everything was working out as per my plans. During the first year of my bachelor's, I'd decided to do my Masters and Ph.D. in California. I like to plan things out five years in advance.

I did nothing but study during those five years in Berkeley. During occasional trips to India, I met some of my school and college classmates, but I never bothered much about them. I always felt that they were all 'wasting' their time back in India. I had this sense of immense belief that *I* was going to conquer some new frontiers. To be frank, I never bothered much to pay attention to what studies, jobs, and other activities they were engaging in.

However, I kept occasional contact with my IIT friend Kumar. He was pursuing his research at M.I.T on the East Coast. Time zone differences, individual passions, and commitments drifted us apart a bit, but we exchanged our professional and personal developments once in a while.

Studies at Berkeley were like a penance for me. The school attracts some of the most exceptional talent and best students across the globe. The professors there are a diverse lot. They were friendly with us while giving deep insights into the intricate subjects they were teaching. I had the passion and hunger to go deeper and deeper into every lecture and learn more than what was being related in class. I spent most of my time outside of the classrooms in the library and Computer Labs.

Thanks to the influence of Grandpa during my early childhood, I had a fascination for mathematics, and it resulted in my interest in Artificial Intelligence (AI). It was quite thrilling to program computers to understand humans.

I started my research on that topic. Within the AI field, a concept known as **machine learning** started taking roots around that time. In the earlier days of AI, we used to formulate all rules and write computer programs. If unanticipated data arrived, or if the rules were not programmed correctly, those early programs would simply fail.

With machine learning, that problem was partially addressed. Computers could understand how humans were using computing systems in their daily processes and could 'learn,' even if the rules were not fully programmed ahead. This ability to learn made them more understanding and gave them the ability to change their innate structures.

For example, while watching a particular movie, machines will recommend a similar, related film. If you buy a book online, on a specific subject, the store will suggest newer books with exclusive offers. These are all a few examples of how companies leverage machine learning in our daily life.

Within no time, my Ph.D. was completed. When I had my graduation ceremony and saw my nameplate, reading "Dr. K Bhamidipati," I felt a sense of achievement and pride. I had a feeling that I could accomplish anything in the world. I am sure those of you who have achieved that feeling will understand the 'high' that I am talking about. In my school days back home, we used to call it 'kick.'

The Natural Language Understanding (NLU) work that I did with AI in my Ph.D. research earned me outstanding name recognition. I emerged out of Berkeley with about twenty peer-reviewed journal articles, five patents, and personal branding: "Krishna's Methodology."

There was no job search. Right on campus, Sun Microsystems, Oracle, Intel, IBM, and others competed for me and offered jobs. I accepted IBM Research Lab's offer, not because of their salary and perks, but because I liked their no-boundaries offer:

You will have no restrictions or goals. Name your budget, continue your AI Research in our Labs in California and guide a few teams on implementing it in our products …

Oh, what a feeling I got when I was reading that offer letter. Dad used to show it off to friends and family.

My friend Kumar told me that he'd accepted an offer at one of the Wall Street companies in New York. I was sure that he would help them radically change their systems and processes with his unique thinking.

And so, my life after campus living started in Cupertino, California, with a small independent home and my first car.

That was also when a minor change occurred in my life—I met Malati. When I first met her, I never imagined that she would change my feelings, direction, and goals. I don't think I understood Malati fully until much later, after our marriage.

Chapter 7 Malati
Hyderabad, India- 1990

I think it was about two years after I joined IBM that I went to Amalapuram, my hometown, when my Tatha was no longer alive. I tried to visit him when he was bedridden, but he insisted that I should visit India only after I finish my Ph.D. His words were the Bible to me. A home without him felt empty. I went and sat near the river banks, which reminded me of childhood, his teachings, and swimming lessons. I teared up with emotion. Memories of his childish pranks and tickling beard made me smile. I was sure that wherever he went, he would be feeling proud of my progress.

Dad had retired but was well settled. Mom told me about why it was about time for me to get married. I did not have many reasons to say no. I did not have any strong opinions about marriage at that time. Marriage was just a part of my journey, a milestone, and I felt that the timing was right.

I found it amusing when mom told me that Malati, the girl she arranged for me to see, would be a perfect companion, as more than ten parameters matched for us. She apparently talked and checked several background attributes through friends and families. I thought that it was AI matching algorithms at work, the human-way, and could not argue much. We went to see Malati and her family. She was doing her history major at Osmania University, Hyderabad.

I have to say it was love at first sight. There was something magical and comforting in her looks. I was mesmerized by her smile, soft tone, and mannerisms. For a strange reason, I felt very calm while talking to her. I hardly asked her about her career aspirations or academic interests. As I said before, those were the days when I used to think that everything other than AI was useless. I did not have any interest or curiosity about her Arts major.

Malati asked me what I did at IBM Research. As soon as she asked that question, I went off into my world and started talking about convolutional neural networks, machine learning, and AI for more than thirty minutes. I was not sure if she fully understood or not, but she smiled beautifully.

"Did you have any steady girlfriends at Berkeley?"

I was taken aback by her question. My life at Berkeley had only revolved around studies. For a minute, I thought if I should lie and talk about some imaginary girlfriends, but decided to be honest.

"No, Malati, my time was dedicated to research during my studies. I had no time outside of that."

She again smiled beautifully. Oh, my heart skipped a beat. For a moment, I felt that her smile had a tone of sadness in it, but I was in no mental state to analyze that sadness then. I was a firm believer at the time that I was the chosen one to change the world. I hope you understand.

The rest of the days went by like a flash. The wedding was in Hyderabad. It was a typical 90's Non-Resident Indian (NRI) arranged marriage. Neither Malati nor I had any say in the list of invitees, ceremonies, or any of the arrangements. Known and unknown people from both sides ended up attending the programs and directing us on what to do for each of those occasions. One of the ceremonies, however, was thrilling. They would drop a ring in a narrow-mouthed brass vessel, and Malati and I had to insert our hands and fight it out to get the ring out. That was the first time we ever touched each other physically, and we could sense that both were trying to make the other win.

I was longing to meet Malati alone in between those rituals but hardly had the time with all those extended families and introductions that we had to go through. She used to appear like an angel in one of those beautiful Indian silk sarees, and even before I could express my appreciation, she would vanish or get surrounded by guests.

The Reception function before the wedding was a real test for legs. We had to sit and stand to wish about three hundred people well and pose for pictures. I was quite embarrassed when Malati's Dad was introducing me to all of his hundred colleagues as 'a busy scientist in the United States, came to India just for two weeks for the wedding.' The actual time of the wedding was at some untimely hour in the wee hours of the morning. I could still remember our sleepy eyes in those smoke-filled rituals.

Among my friends, Saradhi, Kumar, Murthy, Rajani, and about thirty others came to the wedding. At one point, Saradhi tried to grab my attention to tell me about the activities he was doing. He was settled in Amalapuram, working as a math teacher in a primary school there and doing some social service during weekends. I got bored listening to him.

"Krish, can we use your AI technology to accelerate some of the social service programs in India?"

I was hardly paying any attention to him. I felt quite suffocated and thought that they were all still living in a Stone Age with a narrow point of view.

I was thoroughly mesmerized by then with Malati's companionship and was waiting for our freedom and privacy. We came to the US within one week of our marriage. I felt relieved as soon as the flight landed in San Francisco.

Chapter 8 Team, Trailblazers

My new home and car, my work, inspiring bosses, and most importantly, ever-loving Malati made my life memorable. And a little princess, Samantha, arrived into our family as well.

Around 1999, I got an offer from Google, which I could not refuse. Tech companies were just taking off, and Silicon Valley was fast becoming a true trailblazer on multiple fronts. My focus at Google was mostly on artificial intelligence. Within AI, my team and I did most of our work in machine learning and deep learning.

I have to introduce my Google team to you. Sandeep Khurana received a Master's in Economics from Kellogg Business School and joined me as an intern and grew from there. He is an expert in the economic outcomes of technology. He still writes most of my business proposals. As you know, my early education was in my native language, called Telugu, from the southern state of India. Coupled with the British English I grew up with, I struggle to put my point across in some of the business proposals and blogs. Sandeep was born in America and has a decent flair for both technology and American English, a welcome addition to my team.

Dr. Joanna Li, from Stanford University, was a Computer Science major, and Dr. Stella Louis was an Economics major at Harvard. These three are my team leads. Then there is Erlyn, who manages my schedules and keeps us sane.

Sandeep is a fun guy—always pulling legs, flirting, and making practical jokes on all, including on himself. Over a period of time, Sandeep became quite close to Malati and my team as well. Erlyn tells me that Sandeep and Stella have a special relationship, the social dynamics of which I still don't quite understand.

Dr. Li, from my team, on the other hand, is a steady and balanced person, extraordinarily sharp and busy with her work. Even I am impressed with some of the graph databases research she is doing with **neo4j** and other tools.

In those early days, daily life at the office usually involved discussions about our projects and the works of other great people.

Once we huddled around the new Espresso machine, and Stella asked, "Who coined the phrase Artificial Intelligence first, Krish?"

"We could say that Professor John McCarthy was the father of our Artificial Intelligence work. His early work at Stanford laid the foundation for many of our advances today. He coined that term and defined it as 'the science and engineering of making intelligent machines.' His works have paved the way for us to teach machines to recognize objects, understand spoken words, and help in decision making based on data."

"Krish, were there any other AI scientists of repute from your home state in India before you?" Sandeep's passion for Indian heritage and its people is sometimes limitless.

"Sandeep, my work in AI is just a drop in the ocean. A genius who worked for more than fifty years at Stanford and Carnegie Mellon was Dr. Raj Reddy, who started the Robotics Institute. Coming from India, Raj Reddy was the first person out of Asia to achieve the Turing Award, the highest honor one could get for work accomplished in Computer Science. Raj Reddy is a Padma Bhushan award recipient, the highest civilian honor from India."

"I can probably list about a hundred more people of all origins across the world who made a difference to the field of AI. Your question gives me a thought to write a blog series on this topic to recognize the works of those great people."

We had a new group of interns joining our New College Graduates (NCG) program. Recruiting fresh college graduates from various disciplines and nurturing them with focused programs used to be a hallmark of our growth. These new college graduates gave us diversity across age, race, and thinking. Even though they all had formal backgrounds, I used to spend initial time with them to explain the terminology and fundamental concepts so that all were on the same page.

"Team, welcome to the Research Labs. You will have a great time here. We use the terms; Artificial Intelligence, Machine Learning, and Deep Learning quite often in our discussions. Let me elaborate on some of these terms with examples so that we are all speaking the same language."

"You all know how John McCarthy, the father of AI, defined Artificial Intelligence. Machine Learning is a part of Artificial Intelligence. Even when not coded with all the rules, these machine language systems can learn and change their behaviors. It sounds strange, but these systems are similar to how children grow in their learning, based on various experiences that they encounter. Based on the data points that are emerging, these Machine Learning computers can improve their accuracy over a period of time in doing their tasks."

"Another concept within Machine Learning is Deep Learning, which has dramatically advanced the field of AI. These systems can create a variety of synthetic data and scenarios themselves and verify their outcomes for accuracy. They can do this both with trained data and new data. Based loosely on how the

41

brain's neural network operates, these programs typically need much more significant and robust computing power."

"The processing power used for Deep Learning is powered by Graphical Processing Units (GPUs). Hardware technology also has rapidly advanced over this period. Companies such as NVIDIA are providing highly powerful and cost-effective GPU power to improve the Deep Learning applications."

"Identification of pictures, pattern recognition, natural language understanding, and other complex applications are leveraging Deep Learning today."
I paused to let them take this all on.

"Now, I only explained a few important keywords. Please refer to the reading material that you got during the onboarding and ask your team leads if you have any questions. That's a wrap for this session. Welcome to the Labs."

Chapter 9 Encounter
Hyderabad, India- January 2015

I got an invitation to give a keynote speech on AI from one of the AI conference organizers in India. After my parents had passed away, I'd reduced my trips to India, but I reluctantly accepted the invite and made the journey.

I landed at Hyderabad after several years of being away.

I was booked at the Novotel hotel. The conference organizers came early in the morning and took me to the Gachibowli HITEX Conference Hall in a luxurious car. The town had developed quite a bit over these ten years. Several high-rise buildings, posh roads, and shopping malls lined the streets. There had been no such development during my college days.

India had taken good advantage of the technology wave and progressed economically into a powerhouse.

At the conference, attendees listened to every word I said, raptly and with pin-drop silence. I explained how data was going to be pervasive in our daily lives, why data was initially thought of as the new oil, and how AI was going to teach us new ways of doing our work with that data, all with examples.

The audience was enthralled and applauded several times during my speech. I gave my crystal ball on how far AI could go—the impact it would have on our future lives, and how to learn to program these AI systems. The response I got was outstanding.

"Any questions?" As soon as I paused and asked, about twenty people raised their hands.

"Dr. Krishna, my name is Dipika Soni. I am an engineer at Microsoft, Hyderabad. I have two questions. In your blogs, you frequently talk about contextual AI. Can you elaborate? Secondly, do you think data is still the new oil?"

"Please, call me Krish. Nice questions. I will try to explain in a simpler *context*—pun intended." Big laughter sounded throughout the room.

"Every day and in each moment, we come across hundreds of data points. Based on the context we are at, our brain takes only the relevant parts of that data and gives us a cognitive direction. Computers with that kind of intelligence are called contextual AI systems."

"For example, when you get into your car in the morning, your phone understands that you are going to the office at that time and suggests a new route for you to take based on traffic, weather, and the next meeting schedule. The application on your phone in this example has understood your context to give proper guidance," I concluded.

"And Dipika, as per your second question, I would say contextual understanding of data is the new oil. Unlike oil, data can be used multiple times without loss. However, systems that leverage the proper understanding of that data in the context of the consumer's needs are the real winners."

Another person spoke up. "Krish, my name is Mallika Arora from Saama Technologies, India. We feel inspired that you have done so much patent-worthy work. Can you explain some of your recent patents in a language that we can understand?"

"Mallika, in the limited time we have, I will pick a couple of recent innovations that have broad applicability to explain."

"The first one is a work that our team did with Natural Language Understanding (NLU) for scrubbing the Protected Health Information, also known as PHI data, of patients. To identify patients to run clinical trials using Real-World Evidence data, we sometimes need to analyze doctors' notes about their patients. In such cases, we have to carefully remove and de-identify all protected information of patients using NLU. This particular work leveraging Deep Learning techniques got us several accolades and a patent."

"Another interesting project that is near and dear to me is the advanced research we are doing in the genomic vector space. The drugs given to patients participating in clinical trials work for some but do not for others. To understand the groups for which the drug works, the traditional methods of using lab and other results are not sufficient for precision medicine. We need to integrate genomic and multi-omics data and analyze the genomic vector space of patients. This is an exciting new area where data, technology, AI, and clinical sciences all come together."

I paused and took a sip of water. "I guess I am going a bit too deep into the subject. Please read my blogs and detailed whitepapers on these topics for further clarity. For now, let's lighten things up a bit. Any more questions on the broader understanding and applicability of AI that I can explain?" I wanted the more general audience who'd come to listen to my keynote to ask their questions, not just the technically trained folks.

"Can this contextual AI predict and tell me what my wife's mood will be like today?" The room roared with laughter at the question.

"Even though you asked that as a joke," I replied, "it is a very complicated question. Change of moods, laughter, feelings are easily handled and responded to by human brains. However, to program computers to do those simple things that brains do is still a long way away. We are making baby steps in AI," I explained.

"To teach tasks to computers that humans can do easily, you have to spend billions of dollars. Ten percent of unnecessary AI research can solve the fundamental water problem for ten thousand of my village people."

The conference hall went silent as that passionate voice called out. It continued, "My name is Saradhi. I am a primary school teacher in Amalapuram."

"What is the social benefit of your AI for society? Can you give an honest answer?"

I took another sip of water. I would usually answer any complex or deep question about AI without even blinking. But now, I was taken aback like a deer in the headlights. Not because of the depth of that question, but because of who had asked it. My childhood friend, Saradhi, was fearless, direct, and to the point.

I don't even remember what response I gave. It was a wrong note and an unpleasant ending to an otherwise excellent keynote speech. I felt as if everyone in the audience was asking me the same question: "What is the social benefit of AI?"

As soon as I got down from the stage, several people circled me for autographs and introductions—some of the top CEOs, Managing Directors, and executives at several large companies in India. My eyes, however, noticed Saradhi in that group, making his way to me. Saradhi, with a simple khaddar shirt and loose pants.

"I am seeing you after several years, Krishna. Hope Malati and kids are doing well." As he approached and started talking, everyone was eyeing us with interest. I reluctantly gave him a handshake.

"Krishna, can you give me one hour of your time? I need to tell you about some of the work that I am doing in our village to brainstorm."

"Glad to see you, Saradhi. I have some urgent appointments to attend to after this session. Please send me those details via email. I will surely read and respond." I hurriedly left the room and the crowd.

If you think my above behavior toward him was arrogance, I didn't care. Insulting me with an uncomfortable question in front of hundreds of people and reaching out to me with warm overtones made me irritated. If the world made a top-five AI scientists list, my name would be among them. Didn't I have a right to have some ego?

Chapter 10 Malati

Cupertino, USA- January 2019

I rapidly acquired a respectable name and fame for my work at Google. Understanding the human behaviors and actions of various domain experts was one of the critical goals of my early AI projects. Once the systems understood and were programmed into thinking machines, I felt that we could replicate millions of knowledge-workers easily.

"If you create a new world as a competition to nature's creation, you will be in Trishanku, Mr. Krishna Vishwamitra," was the line of argument that Malati used to have with me about my work. She was referring to Saint Vishwamitra, who created a new world called Trishanku Swarga for one of his disciples, defying the Gods' will.

Malati's anguish was that while AI had its benefits, it would eliminate blue-collar jobs for a large number of people out there. Even though she had some merit in her argument, my thinking was that no one could stop this progression of AI from changing our way of life. She would not give up her arguments with me on this topic.

"What about haves and have-nots, Krish? America and the Western world are attracting experts like you to rule the world. What about the poorer countries that do not have access to that intellect and infrastructure? Is it not intellectual colonization?"

"No, Malati, your fears are ill-conceived. Every piece of advanced work that we are doing is in the public domain. Did you not read *The World Is Flat* by Tom Friedman? Today, anyone in the world can leverage these technologies and advancements. The rest of the world is progressing way more than what you are imagining."

"Do not be happy by just putting a few parts in the open domain, Krish. Like colonists in the British Empire ruled the world, Facebook, Amazon, Apple, Netflix, and Google are ruling the world now with intellectual superiority. You are trying to hide behind Tom Friedman's view that the world is flat, but the real question is, is there a true level playing field now on which the world can compete? Don't you see the stranglehold that corporate America has on the world today?" she asked.

I was getting exasperated.

"So what do you want us to do, Malati? Should we all stop our research until the rest of the world catches up? Your left-leaning socialist theory will take us backward. History has already taught us that."

"You are going back to your comfort zone again, Krish. Be honest, and tell me. Without the multi-billion dollars in corporate funding you have, can you honestly say that you could do all your research? All I am asking is to create a level playing field."

She took a deep breath and continued. "Moreover, please come out of your America-Silicon Valley-Google-AI bubble. I doubt you know much of the real world beyond your work and products."

I was awestruck when Malati expressed her point of view with a simple example and a call for action. She pointed out my cocoon and the bubble in which I lived. She was right. I hardly cared or read about things beyond my projects, team, and home. Even though I did not fully endorse her views about the progression of AI, I did not have enough data to counter her. My ego did not allow me to concede the argument, but I had to admit to myself that her ideas were indeed progressive. I felt so proud at that moment that Malati was my life partner. Yes, I decided, I should think more about creating a universal, level playing field for AI.

Chapter 11 Scientist or Reformer?

Cupertino, USA- January 2019

"What boss, you look distracted. Did you lose yet another argument with Malati at home?" Only Sandeep at the office had the closeness to question me like that. I explained Malati's point of view to him.

"Sandeep, even though there is some credence to Malati's argument, I feel that she has not understood the true value proposition of this technology revolution. Don't we see a tremendous progression across the world from all walks of life, thanks to AI research?"

"Okay, Krish, let me hear you out. Can you give me a few examples of the change and progression that you are talking about?"

As soon as Sandeep asked, "Netflix, Amazon, Google" came onto my lips.

"Krish, that's a joke. Using AI, Netflix is successfully promoting movies that I would not have seen before. Amazon is making me buy interesting but excessive items. And Google is learning from our search patterns and is making hay with advertisements. I guess all of these are thanks to your AI recommendation engines?"

"When I asked you to name social benefits due to AI, why do you give me nothing but materialistic examples, Krish?" said Sandeep.

Were global corporations exploiting human intellect? Was I also adding fuel to that same fire?

However, I was not a social reformer. I was an Artificial Intelligence scientist. My responsibility was to use my knowledge and intellect to advance the works that I was doing, and not to think of social benefits. With that firm thought process, I explained my stance to Sandeep.

"Sandeep, I strongly feel that as AI technicians, our job is to advance the sciences and let people across all walks of lives use technology to improve their productivity. If we get entangled in the applications and usage of AI, we cannot further the research."

"Krish, maybe you have a point. Let us see this problem from your side then. Can you list out ten major events or periods in AI that have made a major impact on people?" Sandeep's probing question put me in a spot, not because I couldn't come up with the events, but because I had a tough time picking just ten.

"Sandeep, you asked a tough question. I can list a hundred things in AI that have changed our world. But let me see if I can choose a top ten."

I was silent for a moment, then continued. "The AI research that we are enjoying is the work of thousands of people across the globe at several points in time over the last sixty-plus years. Though I'm sure I'll miss a few key events, I will write my top-ten list on this whiteboard:"

	Time	Event	Impact
1	1950	TURING TEST	Measuring intelligence
2	1955	DEFINITION OF AI	Knowing the boundaries of AI
3	1964	ELIZA	Man-machine interactions
4	The70s	AI WINTER	Period of rethinking and solutions for big business such as RI
5	1997	DEEP BLUE	Chess champion humbled by a machine
6	2002	ROOMBA	AI to clean our homes
7	2011	WATSON	Jeopardy champion humbled by a machine
8	2014	ALEXA	We got used to talking to machines
9	2017	ALPHAGO	Go game champion humbled by a machine
10	2018	DALIA	Clinical research reimagined

"Sandeep, this is by no means a complete list of key events, and I probably missed a few. I, however, feel that I've made my point."

"Thanks, Krish. Your list looks awesome. What do you mean by AI Winter in Point #4? Was there a collective vacation back then?" asked Sandeep.

"That period of the 1980s to 1990s was an interesting time, an era that several historians pinpoint as the AI Winter. The end of that period was when commercial value started to be realized, attracting renewed investments. The first commercial expert system called RI came out then from Digital Corporation. Also, 'bottom-up' thinking as an approach for AI and the entire field of neural networks emerged out of that winter, thanks to the pioneering paper 'Elephants Don't Play Chess.' You can read more about it online."

"You also are very familiar with the other items I listed, including ALPHAGO and the virtual assistants. These Deep Learning intent learning virtual assistants are redefining access and understanding of data across industries. Think of the impact and applications they would have. For example, to patients waiting for a doctor in a remote town or to support staff in improving their productivity. If you are not convinced that AI work is not making an impact on the people, I can't convince you anymore," I concluded.

These discussions with Sandeep lightened my heart and refocused my purpose. I brushed aside the thoughts seeded by Malati and became busy again with my projects. Time moved quite fast with my busy and exciting work.

In less than ten years at Google, I'd climbed multiple ladders and was probably one of the few to get promoted into a Senior Vice President role so quickly. At that time, you might have been using several applications daily that my team had designed and developed. When our CEO gave a live demonstration of the Virtual Assistant that my team built, I felt a great sense of pride and satisfaction. When the execs of your company demonstrates the product you created to the world, the kick you get is at a totally different level.

While I was at Google, our family grew with our second daughter, Asha. Including our pet, the four girls, Malati, Samantha, Asha, and Millie, dominated the home. Malati, however, had the final word among all of us.

Yes, life both at home and work was bliss during those years.

Chapter 12 Letter-Part1
Cupertino, USA- January 2019

As I said before, those twenty years were a sweet dream. Everything went as I wanted, as per my plans. The arrival of Saradhi's two-page letter was, however, a disturbance—a moment when I questioned my principles.

"Dad, you got a large letter from India. It has all these weird and funny stamps on it."

As soon as I got out of the car, Samantha handed me the letter. I first thought that it was one more junk mail. There were always some letters or other pieces of mail asking me for either charity donations or inviting me to give speeches at conferences. I reluctantly opened that letter while still standing in the garage.

"2019 January
Krishna,

For several years, I have wanted to share my activities and brainstorm with you. I have been following every significant project that you have been doing over the years. Every step of yours fascinates me. Yes Krish, I have been saving your every article, blog, and whitepaper in my files.

I've admired you since childhood. Lord Krishna has given us the direction and principles of life through his Gita. However, my friend Krishna has proven that God-given intelligence can be mechanized, and our journey can be simplified. You are no less than the real Krishna for me.

However, Krish, have you noticed what is going on around us? Your company is probably earning billions of dollars with your work. You can justify that your research is getting published in the public domain and GitHub. I am not finding fault with your employer, but what about the basics of "Do No Harm with Technology" principles? I heard that your American military uses your AI works in some large projects. Is the intention to become a bigger brother to the world than what you are already today?

Biology research is another headache. I read that someone created a cross between a pig and a sheep using some of your research elements. It was gut-wrenching to read it. What happened to all the talk of ethical AI?

I never imagined that you would one day become an Einstein and turn out to be a catalyst for destruction.

Why not direct your AI research to identify drugs for rare diseases? I understand that there are no medicines for 90 percent of known illnesses. Can't you lead the use of your AI to develop those drugs?

And what about the underrepresentation of socially disadvantaged classes of people to participate in clinical studies? Can't you solve at least part of that problem with your advanced technology?

Why not do AI research to reduce drug development timelines and costs? I recently read that Pharma companies spend about three billion dollars and take more than five years to bring out one drug. Can't you change that state of affairs?

Or help patients in clinical care with AI?

Krish, in our native village, Amalapuram, people are struggling to buy medicines. These are your American companies' patented drugs. They are at the same price in US dollars in your country as well as here, due to unified pricing policies. But the people here still earn their income in Indian Rupees. How can they afford those treatments?

I neither have the domain understanding nor the intellectual depth to preach to you. My thoughts are all from just bookish knowledge, mostly acquired by reading your blogs and by observing the plight of people around me. I am sure you are getting bored with my criticism. I am not even sure if you have patiently read this far. Let me come to the point of why I started writing this letter to you.

I need an urgent personal favor from you for a program that I am working on. I sold off my house, provident fund, and other savings, but I am still short of ten lakh rupees. My wife, Radha, never objected to any of my social activities. If I don't have at least ten lakh rupees, I can't complete the program that I want to do. We can save the lives of ten thousand people, Krish. I am attaching a detailed project plan on what I want to do with that money.

Let me repeat shamelessly: I need the money urgently. Can you arrange to send it?

Give my respects to Malati and best wishes to the kids.
Your best friend,

Saradhi
PS: Project plan attached."

Chapter 13 Krishna vs. Krishna

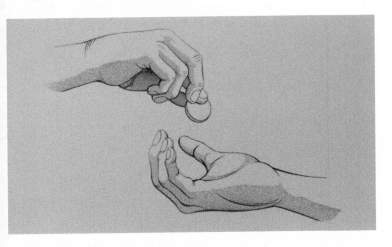

I got irritated before I had read half of the letter. The moment I saw 'ethical AI,' I became thoroughly annoyed. The discussion of the moralities of technology had become a fashion these days. Every Tom, Dick, and Harry was talking about the fundamentals of AI research, saying, "Do No Evil." Now somebody who had been wasting his time in a remote village in Amalapuram was also questioning my work. How ridiculous.

However, some guilty feelings made me not trash that letter. Irritated, I left that half-read and ill-understood note in my bedroom drawer. If only I'd completed reading and understood the intent of that full letter, this story would have been different.

I completely forgot about it, though, and became busy again with my usual work. I had a significant software release to complete, and I had no time to think of anything else.

Not every Krishna is a Krishna.

Chapter 14 Level Playing Field Revisited
Cupertino, USA- April 2019

One weekend, when I was working at my home office, Samantha came over to me for help with her essay. She was writing a positioning paper on the role of technology in human productivity. I was pleased that she'd taken up that topic. I'd given her several impactful examples during our dinner conversations the previous night and was expecting her to narrate them in her own style. She was a young adult, slowly maturing into her own identity.

"Dad, I read some of the articles and references you gave me, but I am not convinced that they substantiate the point I wanted to write about the impact of technology. I need some help," said Samantha shyly.

"Sure, sweetheart, what do you want to know specifically? From the early twentieth century to our current times, I can explain how technology and AI have been changing our lives."

"Well, the main topic I chose for this paper is to research and highlight the positive impact of technology and AI on Black Americans in this century. Unfortunately, the data that I am seeing is not helping my hypothesis."

"What do you mean, Samantha? Technology has no color. Black, white, brown—how does it matter? Why are you bringing race into this equation?" I said, a bit surprised.
"Oh, Dad, I wish it were so simple. Look at some basic facts that I collected." She waved me over to take a look at her document on the laptop.

"You can see that from the information I gathered from various sources that the data is tilted against the Black community in terms of the opportunity to take advantage of the technology revolution and its benefits that you talk about. For example, in this chart that I built from the NCSES website, you can see that for the year 2017, only 3% of Blacks were awarded Ph.D. in the USA in the fields of science, technology, and math. The number of Ph.Ds awarded to Blacks in math and computer science was less than 2%."

I didn't know what to say to that.

"And Dad, when I dig deep to find out why Black Americans do not get enrolled in or pursue these advanced degrees in proportion to their population, I find some disturbing results."

She continued, "The odds to succeed are not equal for Black Americans, Dad. Let me read out some points,

"A brilliant black professor was questioned if she had a doctoral degree. She was mistaken for a janitor. Statistics show that Black faculty are more likely to be denied tenure compared to their white colleagues. That's not even talking about underlying inequalities in healthcare, economics, and other social factors." She paused.

Samantha's research was bothering. I'd never thought about racial inequalities or society's imperfections as factors in the technology world. While the technology and AI revolution were happening in this century, had society locked some people out?

I remembered the shameful imperfections of the social fabric during my childhood, and how subsequent measures gave special privileges to the disadvantaged, ranging from education to economic benefits. A radical approach is indeed needed in the USA to change what Samantha made me realize. Maybe they needed to be given tools and facilities to leapfrog from there? Her assignment and research work definitely left me disturbed.

In times like these, I would call upon my college mate, Kumar. Though sometimes we would not talk for months or even years, I could start a conversation at any time on any topic with him. It was about 11 p.m. on the East Coast, but I picked up the phone and called him.

"Kumar, I need some help. Samantha tells me that Black Americans have far lesser chances to get a higher education, leave alone doing a Master's or Ph.D. in Computer Sciences. What can we do to change that? I want to give some ideas to Samantha on this topic for her paper," I asked, without giving him much preamble.

"Krish, firstly, it is 11 p.m. out here, and I was trying to get to sleep. However, what Samantha is asking is so close to my heart that I am going to give you a hundred things that we need to do to radically change the social imbalance," said Kumar.

That's what I like about him. He is not only a brilliant engineer but also can connect the dots across horizons. I was all ears trying to absorb his insights.

"First and foremost, it all starts with primary education in STEM. We have to incentivize the underprivileged to give them access to STEM education at a minimal cost. Teaching in shelters, YMCA, and other troubled areas would have a wider reach. The teachers can be high school students, college teachers, and employees of tech companies. Some existing online programs can be scaled for broader reach. Secondly, making affordable hardware and software accessible for experimental research is essential. Only the rich and privileged have access to advanced classes such as Robotics, etc. right now. We have to break that cycle."

"And, Krish, if you call me up at a saner hour, I can give you more detailed plans and blueprints. Please remember that there is a three-hour time difference between us," he admonished me sleepily.

"Thanks, Kumar. You gave me enough pointers, for now, to help Samantha with her report. Go back to bed, buddy."

I sat with Samantha again, and we both worked on her paper with some ideas and conclusions. I felt enlivened with the new lens that Samantha made me see the world through, and the ideas that Kumar had explored.

Chapter 15 Spring Cleaning
Cupertino, USA- October 2019

"I need help at home from you, Krish. Can you make sure that you don't have weekend meetings or calls?"

Malati hardly ever interrupted my schedules and work. Listening to her small request amused me. It was true that almost every day, I had some meeting or another across time zones with my global teams. I texted Erlyn and asked her to clear up my weekend calendar. Without asking any questions, she just replied, 'It's done.' That took care of one problem.

"What is the program this weekend, Bujji? Any special guests coming from India? I am fully at your service. Erlyn is clearing up my schedule and blocking my time."

I knew that whenever I called her "Bujji," she would melt. Back when email communications were not pervasive, in my handwritten letters when I was in a good mood, Bujji was my favorite name by which to address her. Shall I tell you what she used to call me when she was in a good mood? Sorry, that is our private matter.

Malati's face was lit like a thousand candles, as I expected. It had been a while since I'd seen that glow in her face. I got more satisfaction seeing her happiness than what I would get from solving a complex nth-order parametric equation. Was I losing the real joy of life because I was too caught up at work?

"We are doing spring cleaning this weekend, Krish. Our goal is to clean every room, closet, and nook and corner of the house. If we have not used an item during the last six months, we will set it aside to donate it to Goodwill. Junk is piling up. I am getting sick of seeing our excesses. I also told the kids to clean up their rooms. I am so glad that you are helping me out this weekend."

Malati certainly had a generous heart. Under the disguise of cleaning, she would pick up all our duplicate items, unused clothes, and kitchen stuff and take it to the Goodwill store for distribution to the poor. She usually managed this work herself and rarely asked me to help.

I was becoming mesmerized by her organizational skills while cleaning up each room. Her approach to completing the chores, decision-making command, and task management were impressive. I didn't often see those qualities, even among some of my teams.

"Krish, tell me which of these shoes you are not going to use anymore."

When Malati asked that simple question, it reminded me of the difficulties we would face with Classification algorithms. I acquired all of those shoes at various points in time, out of varied interests. Friends gifted some; I purchased some of them to remember the places I visited; I bought some of them because I liked a particular style. How would I do a simple Linear Separation and tell which ones I liked and which ones I didn't? I was thinking of how to solve that complex problem.

I got a jolt when Malati said, "You are not going to use these four pairs, and I am putting them aside." How did she solve a third-order deep learning neural network problem so fast?

"Wow, when did you learn deep learning, Malati? How did you compute the error function so quickly?"

Malati laughed endlessly at my innocuous question.

"Deep Learning, my foot. I have been observing you for the last two years. You'll take these out and then put them aside. I have not seen you wear them up for any occasion, with any outfit. I don't need your AI programs for that decision. Simple common sense, my dear Watson."

I did not miss the pun on IBM and Sherlock Holmes. Though humbled, I had to admire her sense of humor. What Malati said reminded me of the lectures I would give on supervised and unsupervised learning. I was a big proponent of intent learning techniques, which Deep Learning models use to improve their inference. What Malati explained was no less.

As I mentioned earlier, did I understand Malati fully? What did she study? That minute, I felt that she studied life.

On Sunday morning, groggy, I heard her voice. "The last room left is your library. Our spring cleaning will be done by this Sunday. Wake up, Krish."

When Malati woke me up with loud fanfare, I felt that the weekend was ending too soon. How silly. I was always looking forward to Mondays, to rush to the office and tackle the next big thing at work. I never realized that I would get a bigger kick while sharing household chores with Malati.

I raced to my library room. I wanted to enjoy every moment with Bujji this weekend.

But I instantly realized that something was wrong when I tapped her back and asked, "Where do we start?"

I had never seen a teared-up Malati like that, ever. Fear shivered through my spine.

"Are you okay, Bujji? What happened?"

"I am okay, Krish. The real question is, are you okay?" Her voice rose as she spoke to the point she was nearly screaming.

I did not understand her at all. In our years of married life, Malati had never shouted at me like that.

There was a multi-page letter fluttering in her hands. Had someone from her family fallen sick? Who the hell wrote letters these days?

"How can you be so selfish, Krish? Are you a human being or a senseless AI machine? How could you not respond to such an earnest request?" said Malati, throwing that letter at me.

I remembered the letter that I'd half-read and hurriedly stashed away in my library months ago. To hell with it. Malati was too sensitive about these matters, I felt.

But I sank into my chair and started reading the letter.

Chapter 16 Letter-Part2
Cupertino, USA- October 2019

"2019 January
Krish,

....

Your best friend,
Saradhi

PS: Project Plan attached."

After re-reading those first two pages with sincerity, I could hear my heart thumping. With moist eyes, I moved on to the remaining unread pages.

Free Drug Depot Project

"Krish, it is not just our village. Most of the poor people from our neighboring communities are unable to buy medicine. I strongly felt that I had to do something for them and did some research. I found out that many drugs get wasted in the world. Sometimes, these are bought and unused by those who can afford it. My idea is to make a systemic process to collect those unused drugs and distribute them to the needy.

My idea is to start a 'Free Drug Depot for the Needy.' As per my calculations, even in our village, about a thousand people can be helped with such a facility. I don't have the reach to save the world. All I want is to protect our village.

Even with the minimum budget, I need at least ten lakh rupees. It is laughable. Forget about lakhs. I don't have even ten thousand rupees in my bank.

Why am I writing this to you? In addition to financial help, I know that you could use your brains to expand my program.

If you can't spend time, at least send me the much-needed ten lakhs. I am not saying this to make you feel bad, but do you remember Venkat Rao, our high school watchman who used to give you raspberries during lunch breaks? He recently passed away with cancer.

The unfortunate thing is, his disease had a remedy, but his poverty did not.

All I am hoping for is to save a thousand people like him. I am hoping
that you will call me as soon as you read this letter.

Yours
Saradhi"

I'd never wept this much in my lifetime, not even when Mom
passed away. The letter became drenched with my tears. I
found myself lying on Malati's lap, incessantly crying for a
while.

All of my titles, fame, patents, degrees, and victories appeared
useless and pale. More importantly, the feeling that Malati must
be treating me as a greedy machine with no values was
upsetting. How could I convince her that I was not that selfish?
I got up and took out the phone to talk to Saradhi, but Malati
stopped me.

"It is too late, Krish. As soon as I read this letter, I started
making calls. He left the village with his family. He could not
sustain his Free Drug Depot and could not face the hopeless
people lining up for his help. There are rumors that he
committed suicide."

I was going into an endless pit now. Was Malati now attributing
his death to me? Was I that bad a person?

"Saradhi thought that you were a technological incarnation of
Lord Krishna. Just like Kuchela reached out to his friend,
Krishna, for help, he reached out to you as a last resort. Even

that was not for his own gain. We don't even have half an hour to spare for our childhood friends. We are the stereotypical Americanized Western machines disguised as humans. The ten lakhs he asked for is less than the two-day expenses of our last Hawaii trip. I guess we have to live with this guilt for the rest of our whole lives."

Every word that Malati uttered was piercing me like a bullet. My childhood memories with Saradhi all came back: those swims across the backwaters, college studies, philosophical differences, and fights, all of it flooded my mind.

Was I jealous of his value system and unselfish motives? Was that the reason why I did not pay attention to him? What if I had offered some help either when I met him at the Hyderabad conference or when I first read that letter—would that have rescued him?

I also had a sinking feeling that I had let down my Tatha and the values he instilled in me. He taught me to remember my friends and extend help to them when asked. Instead, I ignored the call for help. My daughter Samantha's term paper on the inequalities of technological benefits in society, and her subtly pointing out what I could do, came to my mind as well. I'd just had blinders to my inner eye so far.

The thought that I might have killed my childhood friend was killing me. But on further thinking, I felt that Saradhi was not a coward. He had strong convictions and beliefs in his principles. I was sure that somewhere, he would be safe and sound, doing some good work for someone in his way.

I could feel that he was alive—my heart was telling me that.

I could use my money, name, and influence to find out where he was right now. I could ask for his forgiveness and offer him help. I started thinking about how to locate him and had a sudden flash of insight.

The problem here was not just of one Saradhi and one Krish. Helping Saradhi alone was not a solution when there are millions of well-intentioned people like him in the world, and all of them need a helping hand.

In the mythological story, a childhood friend of Lord Krishna, named Kuchela, went out to Krishna seeking help, and Krishna obliged. Kuchela had a happy ending there.

However, today, hundreds of Kuchela-like Saradhis do not know who or where the helpings hands of Krishnas are in the world.

What if I used the power of Artificial Intelligence to connect these two groups of people? Those who needed help to scale their social programs and those who could help? Just like startups got resources from crowdfunding, these smaller social programs across the world would get financing from interested people across the world, not from politicians and governments.

Anyone in the world embarking on a good deed would get connected to thousands of Lord Krishnas to help. It would ensure visibility, financial stability, expansion, and scalability of such good social programs.

A technical design to build a platform for social programs with peer-to-peer networks started emerging in my mind. We use Facebook today to connect with friends and families across the world. We use WhatsApp groups to share related interests. Similar to that, we could use this new platform to focus on social programs across the world and get connected.

Once I started looking at the problem through this lens, I became re-energized with the strength of a thousand elephants. My teams have designed and built highly scalable AI applications and platforms that are being used every minute by millions of people. I had the confidence that I could use the same techniques to conceptualize, scale, and solve this problem.

Unknowingly and knowingly, both Saradhi and Malati made me realize my North Star and showed me a path to get there.

"Bujji, thanks for opening up my inner eye. I now understand the journey that I need to embark upon and my ultimate goal. Finding and helping just our dear Saradhi is not my sole aim. Identifying thousands of such people, giving visibility to their programs, and expanding their outcomes to millions is my responsibility.

"But honey, I'm sorry for breaking my word. I need to head back to the office right away."

"I am going to resign from Google, come out of my comfort zone, and build a startup with a purpose. My new company name is KUCHELA.AI."

Malati understood my goal and gave me a hug.

Chapter 17 Planning
San Francisco, USA- January 2020

"Krish, are you okay? We are waiting to hear from you."

Like I just received a jolt, I come out of my trance.

"Sorry team, I was just thinking about how to explain the problem statement of our new project. Let me explain."

"There are several great people in this world who are using their creativity and ideas to start social service programs within their capacity. However, due to their limited resources, those programs are not giving the intended results. Most of them die early on. Even those who succeed have a limited reach."

"Our goal is to expand the reach of those social programs by increasing visibility across all corners of the world. We will connect the missing dots among the creators of those good social programs and resources. We will ensure proper governance and sustainable infrastructure to expand and reach the needy across the world.

"Our project name is KUCHELA.AI. Any questions?"

I can immediately see ten raised hands. I wave Dr. Li to ask first.

"Krish, great concept. I can see how I could use a graph database to design the application. But what is that name, KUCHELA.AI? What does it mean? Or is it one of your riddles?"

"No, Li. It is not a riddle. That name is an inspiration for our work. I have to tell you a short story to explain why I arrived at that name."

"In Hindu mythology, there were two childhood friends named Krishna and Kuchela. They both studied together and shared a great bond. They parted ways after high school. This guy, Krishna, became a famous person, and Kuchela ended up in abject poverty. Long story short, when Kuchela took the courage to reach out to Krishna for assistance, Krishna provided all the help needed to make Kuchela happy."

"These days, there are thousands of good Kuchelas in the world, potentially seeking help, but others who could assist them are not able to hear their pleas."

"We will use the power of AI to solve that problem globally."

"Oh, dear friend, tell me what you got for me."

Someone in the room is playing an old Telugu language song on YouTube, which narrates the story of Lord Krishna and Kuchela. While serious project discussions are going on, only Sandeep plays these pranks to create some humor. Even though I get irritated a bit, I like his spontaneity in finding the right background music and song for our situation.

After seeing my smile, he stands up.

"We are searching for all the poor Kuchelas in the world to let the rich Krishnas help them, right?"

"No, Sandeep, our goal is to bring out the inner Krishnas (or goodness) in each of us and help the social programs to scale. The creators of those programs are the real heroes, not the folks who are helping.

"There is a beautiful poem by an Indian poet named Javed Akthar. It loosely translates to: 'There is a Ram (Good) and Ravan (bad) in each of us. Kill that Ravan and bring out Ram.'

We will use technology to suppress that bad and let good emerge from all."

I put my hands together. "Okay, team, this meeting is over. Dr. Li and Sandeep will lead the technical and business threads. Get your data and thoughts together to discuss the overall design and next steps in a week. No time to waste."

Just I'm about to dismiss the meeting, a critical question is asked.

"What is the overall budget for this project? And what about the timelines?" asks Stella. Without timelines and dollars, she won't let us move forward.

"There is no budget constraint for KUCHELA.AI. I will fund whatever it takes. But, yes, we have a time constraint. I want to take KUCHELA.AI into focus group release within one quarter and release it globally by the end of 2020 to generate real outcomes worldwide."

She nodded, and I addressed the whole room.

"That's a wrap. We will meet at the same time next week."

Chapter 18 Demo
San Francisco, USA- April 2020

It's been about four months since we started the KUCHELA.AI project.

When I saw the calendar invite asking me to attend the prototype demo of KUCHELA.AI, my respect and admiration for the team grew enormously.

I know that with design reviews, brainstorming sessions, weekly sprints, and agile scrum stand-ups, the team has put in countless hours at the office and home over the last few months. Some of them even went for days without sleep. When a talented team works with focus and dedication, I feel that even climbing Mt. Everest would be an easy task.

"Krish, I know that you hate slides, but allow me to show you the concept map on this big screen first before we jump into a demo."

Slideware is the problem with the business school upbringing. Sandeep cannot explain without his PowerPoints.

"No more than five slides, Sandeep, and they better be relevant," I say, a bit impatiently.

The room becomes dark, and the projector lights up.

Slide-1:
KUCHELA.AI
AI-Powered Social Programs

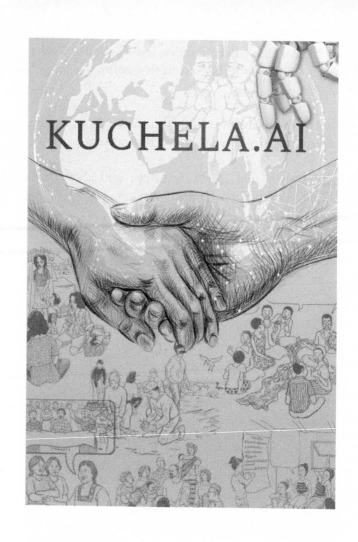

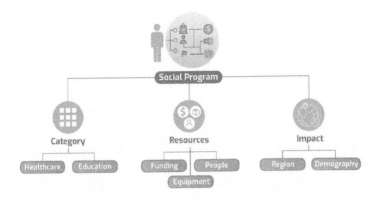

"Social Program is the central node. Every program will have an owner or creator. In our parlance, he is the *Kuchela*.

Category will describe the type of social program such as healthcare, education, culture, etc. Each of the groups will have sub-categories.

Resources are the essential elements to sustain and run the programs. They could be money, equipment, or people. Those people are the *Krishnas,* who would help those programs.

Impact indicates the reach of the program and its effect across demographics."

He continued, "Once we load the global data, we can represent the above in a network graph for better visualization. Kuchela and Krishna here are interchangeable. That means the creator of one social program can be a helper of another program and vice versa. Just like in the Uber paradigm, where a driver and passenger are interchangeable, and the same analogy applies here. Our application is a peer-to-peer network for social programs. Am I making sense so far?"

As Sandeep pauses his explanation, Stella raises her hand.

"Sandeep, your entity diagram and the network graph explanation are clear. What is the meaning of the image you showed in your first slide? It looks very intricate."

"Thanks for asking that great question, Stella. I was dying for someone to ask that. With the suggestions that Krish gave, I struggled with our graphic designer to come up with that theme."

"You will see three hands there in the image. One is the hand of Kuchela, and the second is that of Krishna. The third hand is the invisible technological power of our Artificial Intelligence-based application."

"At the bottom of the hands, we show several social activities. The globe represents that these social programs are across the world, and the kids represent the mythological representation of Krishna and Kuchela during their school days."

"Even though Krish came up with this thought process, it is our graphic designer, Prarthana, who converted it into such a beautiful representation. Let us hear from her. She joined us today on the web conference." Sandeep prompted Prarthana to speak up.

"Team, it is such a pleasure to work on this project. In addition to what Sandeep explained, you will also see a design element with a digital flute in the App. It represents the concept of God and his mystical magic wand helping the world in the form of AI," says Prarthana.

The whole team claps and cheers for her. Prarthana's face lights up with a smile. As I said before, when your team appreciates your work in front of the boss, it is a massive ego booster. Nothing is comparable to that satisfaction at work.

"Krish, we took your phone and downloaded and configured the app with your public profile. Please click on it."

Now I understand why Erlyn took my phone in the morning for a brief moment.

I launch the App and Chromecast it onto the big screen:

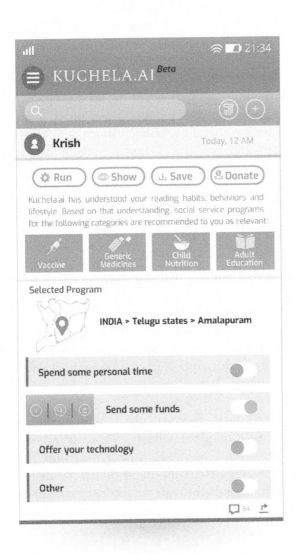

A while ago, I wrote a blog series on how to use AI for compound repurposing to accelerate the development of vaccines for new virus attacks.

In several presentations, I also explained my position on the patent stronghold of pharma and the need for generics.

The App took some of my public material and 'learned' about my interests and direction. Damn science, it appears that AI has no limits on where it can reach.

"We rolled out this beta version to a select focus group of a thousand people, Krish. The response we are seeing is unimaginable."

Another team member, Melinda, takes over the presentation.

"The App identified a water purification program run on a small scale in Uganda. With just ten dollars, they were cleaning ten thousand liters of water. In ten minutes of identifying that social program, our App connected it with five members of our beta program."

"Within ten days, Uganda water purification work got expanded to a hundred villages. There is no clean water shortage in my native village now, Krish. Our focus group team members sent ten thousand dollars to that program's organizers in Uganda through the secured payment gateway we created."

I've never seen Melinda getting so excited about work. I did not know that her native country was Uganda until now. However, after hearing about the fund transfer, I have a concern.

"Melinda, are you sure that the funding sent was well spent? Did our App enable only sending the funds, or also ensure that their use was supervised at the sites? Have you visited that Uganda water purification project site?"

"No Krish, I have been so busy with the work here. I felt that my role was only to design and program this App."

"Melinda, we should be able to prove accountability and good governance for all the programs scaled with our platform. Sending funds is just one part. We also have to make sure that the people who are helping those programs get full visibility and satisfaction. Can you add these features and update your design elements?"

"Yes, Krish, that was a big miss on my part. I see your point. Give me two weeks. I can conceptualize how to use Blockchain and ensure accountability and funding workflows in the design."

"Thanks, Melinda. Team, I see another miss. In our paradigm, the people who could offer help, the Krishnas, can also be corporations. Every company these days has corporate social responsibility program budgets—CSR. We need to link our Kuchelas to those programs. Using peer-to-peer networks, we first search for Krishnas. We then use their CSR budgets. For example, Melinda's presentation reminds me of Singularity University's support for a water desalination program called Naishio. If other corporations are supporting similar programs of our Kuchelas, our engine should interconnect them."

Hearing our discussion, Sandeep seems to realize that I am not yet fully convinced of the completeness of the KUCHELA.AI design.

"Team, from Krish's review comments, I see a few gaps in our design right now. One is program governance, the second is CSR funding, and then there's data integration with other similar programs. We need to brainstorm and add these features in the next sprint. Any other suggestions or feature requests to improve the App?"

Dr. Lee comes forward.

"Sandeep, among us, we have so many good ideas about a few social programs that could help the needy. What if we categorize them from our research and also make them available as a catalog in KUCHELA.AI? It could inspire new social program creators across the world."

I am surprised by her original thinking.

"Excellent suggestion, Lee. I was thinking that the goal of KUCHELA.AI is only to connect existing Kuchelas and Krishnas. Your opinion will pave the way for new Kuchelas to emerge. Along with showing the ideas, we should also include some best practices, tools, and techniques to implement them."

"Let's put some ideas on the board. We can build up a catalog map."

Sandeep compiles all our thoughts on sticky notes, and makes this list on the whiteboard:

Catalog of Social Program Ideas

1. Money lending & soft loans to the needy
2. Connecting terminally ill patients to caregivers
3. Matching economically deprived patients with clinical trials across the world
4. Enabling decentralized manufacturing
5. STEM education and access for underserved populations

"What is that fourth point on decentralized manufacturing, Sandeep? Who gave that idea? Can you elaborate?" asks Dr. Lee.

Sandeep responds before I can. "Oh, some of the catalog ideas came from Krish's friends, during his discussions with them. Krish, you can explain better than me, please go ahead."

I remember the discussions I had with my friend Kumar on this topic.

"Folks, in the USA, and probably across most of the Western world, we have out-sourced our manufacturing needs to low-cost countries such as China. From an economic perspective, that has worked quite well for our people as well as the corporations. However, this single dependency on manufacturing and out-sourcing has several large-scale implications. For example, if the global supply chains break down, during wars or when natural calamities occur, these countries such as China may not be able to supply the goods to us.

"More importantly, due to this continuous out-sourcing, we've lost the ability to produce them locally. Imagine if there is a pandemic? From face-masks to ventilators, we are dependent on Chinese manufacturers to build and supply them."

"However, to come out of this deep hole that we have dug ourselves into requires some radical methods. Traditional processes will not help us solve this situation."

"The maker movement has shown us a path. Companies such as Adafruit have pioneered to prove that using open-source hardware and software, many products can be manufactured at low cost everywhere, without large factories and investments."

"Decentralized manufacturing for the social benefit at scale is the need of the hour." I have to check my deep attachment to this topic and give a pause for people to digest what I said. Sandeep realizes that I'm getting a tad emotional and takes over the summary.

"Thanks, Krish. For every catalog item, our App will give these details. We will provide the design elements, blueprints, and open-source tools that social program creators can optimize locally and take them forward."

"We also need to get the authentic data source feeds into our App for our models to get trained. The accuracy of our social program recommendation engine and a good NLU capability will be critical elements to sustain user interest and value from the App. Remember the fiasco we once had with our Apparel App?" said Sandeep, referring to the failed work we did to recommend to people what style of dresses they could wear based on the specific event they were going to.

I weighed in with my thoughts.

"Sandeep, in that Apparel project, we just did not have enough reliable data for our AI models to get trained on. It was an issue of not having proper ground truth data for the models and also not incorporating a good feedback mechanism within the App. You do make a good point, though. Assign someone to look at ingesting the data of all publicly known social programs and key influencers. This data needs continuous curation as well."

Sandeep nods. "I am summarizing all the action items in the list below. Team, do not forget to prepare the user-stories and design details in Aha, our product management tool. We will meet again next week." He writes the following on the board:

Action Items & To-Do List:

1) Program governance
2) CSR funding integration
3) Catalog of social program ideas
4) Data management and curation
5) Design details for the Catalog

I conclude the meeting and start driving back home. KUCHELA.AI is progressing well. I have the confidence in my team to take it forward. However, some emptiness and dissatisfaction are still bothering me. The person I am searching for, someone that I need to see, talk, and apologize to—Saradhi- is still missing. Where are you, my friend? I know that you are alive somewhere. When will I see you?

Chapter 19 Go-No-Go
San Francisco, USA- April 2020

It has been about two months since we completed the prototype review. The team has been working nonstop with the feedback we gave. I have been attending some of the stand-up meetings and checking the progress. The time has come today to make a Go-No-Go decision. We've assembled as a full team.

"We have rolled out KUCHELA.AI to 1,000 focus group members Krish. The response is outstanding."

Sandeep's face is glowing with satisfaction and pride. He appeared literally to be on cloud nine while showing the demo.

"All the open items that we discussed so far, including governance, CSR funding, and program catalog, are all done and thoroughly tested. I think we are ready for prime-time, Krish."

He continues, "Even with a limited beta roll-out, we've uplifted several good programs worldwide. There is this small nonprofit agency in India which was matching and sending underprivileged patients with rare diseases to clinical trials. Our KUCHELA.AI App learned about that program and connected the program owners with pharma companies here. They got a significant CSR grant to scale."

Sandeep beams. "We might have saved some lives already."
"In addition to enabling a third-party funding grant, we also gave them our technology platform and configured it to their local matching needs. While doing it, we learned quite a few new things and improved KUCHELA.AI algorithms Krish. We can now conclusively say that our technology is solving one of the basic needs of socially disadvantaged and illiterate classes of people to access the advances of clinical research."

Then he looks straight at me. "Another interesting fact; do you know who is organizing that program? Somewhere in a remote district called Idukki in Kerala, this person named S. Yandamoori is running it. I looked at his background and did some digging. It looks like he is also from your hometown in India and the same age group. Do you know him by any chance?"

"His full name is *Saradhi Yandamoori.*"

I feel like crying out loud and laughing hysterically at the same time. The one hope that I sincerely held has come alive in front of me. As I expected, KUCHELA.AI identified and connected an unknown person's good work from a remote place. Moreover, it gave a resource platform for that person to scale that work.

Long live AI technology! I feel that the real value of AI technology has gone up a thousand notches, right here and now.

It's becoming hard to control my emotions. Saradhi's words, *"If you give just ten lakh rupees, I can save a thousand lives, Krishna,"* are reverberating in my ears.

The team is still excitedly explaining the demo and showing off their work. I have to drink a glass of water to get the control to stand up.

I felt a great sense of gratitude—the team worked tirelessly over the past few months. I remember the words I read sometime back in The Alchemist novel, *when you want something, all the universe conspires in helping you to achieve it.* How true.

My life partner Malati, daughter Samantha, friends, and dedicated team all conspired to help me realize my destiny and guided me to reach it.

"Fantastic work, team. It is a go. Please roll it into production immediately. All the backend infrastructure will be on Google cloud." KUCHELA.AI will be a free App to download on all platforms. There will be a $1 subscription fee per month, and all the proceeds we collect from this subscription fee will be sent to the social program of choice."

I continue, "All the App management costs, including DevOps support, infrastructure, and other funding, will be covered from my finances. I am committing one hundred million dollars of personal funds to scale this program. I want us to touch one million people and one thousand social programs within one hundred days."

The team looks shocked. They knew that I have not taken any funding from outside investors, and I am committing all of my net worth towards this project.

Sandeep comes close to me and says, "Krish, are you sure? You know that it is a totally different ballgame to put an application like this into a global rollout. We have proven the concept. With your contacts and reputation, we can easily raise venture money. Why do you have to go all-in for this dream?"

I was touched by Sandeep's empathy and concern, but I was sure of what I wanted to do. I once thought that my sole intention was to advance the sciences, earn money and fame during that process. I now clearly know what my real goal is. The obstacles to achieving that goal are the money, fame, and self-beliefs that I nurtured all these years. I need to cross those obstacles to get to my goal.

"Team, let me repeat our goals: one hundred million dollars commitment, one million people, one thousand social programs, and one hundred days."

I take out a marker and write this on the whiteboard:

Personal Funding: $100,000,000

Reach: 1,000,000 People

Scale: 1,000 Social Programs

Time: 100 Days

"LET'S ROLL

THANK YOU"

Everyone is silent for a few seconds. Once they digest what I said, the room reverberates with claps. I guess Erlyn hears because she comes inside with a big smile and a Champagne bottle.

I am driving back home in a state of Nirvana. I hug Malati and weep with joy as soon as she opens the door. Even she can't control her tears. When you accomplish something substantial, there is no need for any words with your near and dear ones.

But yes, there is one person that I need to talk to. I dial the number that Sandeep gave me. Those seconds of waiting while the phone is ringing are agonizing.

"Hello, who is this?" I listen to the same resounding voice that I was longing to hear and talk to. I have to control my emotions to respond on the phone.

"Hi, Saradhi. This is your Krishna. Can we talk?"

Chapter 20 Award
Oslo, Norway- August 2022

"We now honor a great technologist and philanthropist who used the might of technology and Artificial Intelligence to change the social fabric of the world. With his work broadly known as KUCHELA.AI, millions of people who are doing innovative social services programs across the globe are now connected with thousands of people for support to scale their programs."

"In just two years since its inception, it is estimated that about 100 million people have benefited using the works of Dr. Bhamidipati. His KUCHELA.AI has touched and scaled social programs in healthcare, vaccines, and STEM education, among others, to unprecedented levels. A sustainable social fabric had been stitched together through his works."

"Most importantly, the worldwide pandemic of 2020, COVID-19, found its technological and social match in KUCHELA.AI. We can say that he successfully created a barrier to the spread of the scourge. Thousands of welfare and service programs across the globe got funding and people's support through his App to fight the virus. From ventilators to vaccines, from clinical trials to patient care, his KUCHELA.AI App connected the goodness of people across the world to uplift humanity."

"This year's Nobel Peace Prize is awarded to Turing Award winner, Dr. Krishna Bhamidipati."

While walking up to the stage, I feel Saradhi's words echoing the same thing differently: *I thought that ten lakhs rupee of help from you would help me save a thousand lives, but you used your technology to save millions of people. You fulfilled my life's ambition, Krishna.*

"Honorable Nobel Committee and the distinguished guests; Thanks for conferring this prize on me. I was a strong believer that the sole purpose of any research in technology, AI, and sciences was only to advance those fields. However, my childhood friend, Saradhi Yandamoori, has made me realize that social reform is also a key goal of research and that researchers have a responsibility to make those advances available at low costs to everyone in the world. He has given me completeness to my research."

"On his behalf and on behalf of thousands of such social reformers working tirelessly across the word to uplift human productivity, I am accepting this great honor. Thank you."

Accepting the 2022 Nobel Peace Prize is a great feeling. Equally significant is seeing the people who mean the most to me in the front row—Saradhi, his wife Radha, Malati, Samantha, Asha, Kumar, Sundar Pichai, Suresh Katta, Satya Nadella, Sandeep, Melinda, Li, and others—all giving a standing ovation.

When the work you have done is appreciated by the ones who are near and dear to you that feeling of satisfaction is at an entirely different level.

Epilogue
Amalapuram, India- September 2022

As soon as I touch down to Vijayawada by flight, I take a cab to go to Amalapuram by road. It is a three-hour journey. When I see the 'Welcome to Amalapuram" board, a sense of excitement and calmness comes to me at the same time. I am returning to my hometown after several years. I ask the driver to proceed straight to the river banks. You know who is waiting there for me.

"Saradhi, you asked me, 'What would be the social benefit of AI for society?' I can respond to your question now. Sorry, it took me a while."

"I did not understand you fully either, Krish. Your AI technology has crossed all boundaries in many fields now.

Several tasks have been accelerated and simplified, leading to unprecedented productivity gains, thanks to the work of AI. More importantly, with people like you taking the initiative to get that work into the public domain and open-sourced, there is a level playing field globally now. I am so proud to tell everyone that you are my friend."

"And I am so happy that a Nobel Laureate like you came to inaugurate a small depot in this town." Saradhi shakes my hands with a smile.

The place reverberates with claps and appreciation from the villagers when Saradhi and I cut the ribbon formally to open the 'Free Drug Depot for the Needy.'

I finally feel at home. Their appreciation and admiration give me a sense of satisfaction that is better than what I got from the Turing award in San Francisco and the Nobel Peace Prize in Oslo.

I am sure you understand my feelings.

AI Glossary

AI Timeline

AI Trailblazers

AI Glossary

At several points in this book, technical terms are used contextually. Some of those words are explained here for clarity. Note that contextual liberty with the usage of some terms was taken at times for better readability.

Artificial Intelligence

Artificial intelligence is the science and engineering of making intelligent machines. These AI systems can recognize and identify pictures, understand spoken words and text, and make decisions based on contextual data.

Agile Methodology

This is a type of project management process, mainly used for software development. Demands and solutions evolve through the collaborative effort of self-organizing and cross-functional teams and their customers.

Algorithm

A process or set of rules to be followed in calculations or other problem-solving operations by a computer.

Clinical Trials

Any research study that prospectively assigns human participants or groups of humans to one or more health-related interventions to evaluate the effects on health outcomes.

Cloud Computing
The practice of using a network of remote servers hosted on the internet to store, manage, and process data, rather than a local server or a personal computer.

Convolutional Neural Network
A convolutional neural network (CNN) is a type of artificial neural network used in image recognition, specifically designed to process pixel data.

Crowdfunding
This is a relatively new practice of funding a project or venture by raising many small quantities of money from a large number of people, typically via the internet.

Deep Learning
Deep learning is a subset of machine learning in artificial intelligence that has networks capable of learning unsupervised from data is unstructured or unlabeled. It is also known as deep neural learning or deep neural network.

Deep Mind
DeepMind Technologies Ltd. is a firm based in the United Kingdom that works on artificial intelligence problems. Google has acquired Deep Mind.

DevOps

DevOps (development and operations) is an enterprise software development phrase used to mean a type of agile relationship between development and IT operations.

Error Function

A loss function measures the **error** in a neural network. One of these, for example, is the Mean Squared **Error**, which will calculate the distance between the wanted input and the real input, squaring this value.

Go-No-Go

A decision process to proceed with or abandon a plan or project.

Infrastructure

Information technology infrastructure is defined broadly as a set of information technology (IT) components that are the foundation of an IT service, typically physical parts (computer and networking hardware and facilities), but also various software and network components.

Machine Learning

Machine learning is an application of artificial intelligence (AI) that provides systems the ability to learn and improve from experience without being explicitly programmed. Machine learning focuses on the development of computer programs that can access data and use it to learn for themselves.

NCSES
The National Center for Science and Engineering Statistics (NCSES) is the leading provider of statistical data on the U.S. science and engineering enterprise.

P2P Network
Stands for "Peer to Peer." In a P2P network, the "peers" are computer systems connected via the internet. Files can be shared directly between systems on the web without the need for a central server. In other words, each computer on a P2P network becomes a file server as well as a client.

Platform
A platform is a group of base technologies upon which other applications, processes, or technologies get developed.

Patient Matching
Clinical trial matching services facilitate patient enrollment in clinical trials by identifying potential trials for patients and their proxies.

Rare Diseases
A rare disease is one that affects fewer than 200,000 people. Rare diseases have become known as orphan diseases because most drug companies are not interested in adopting them to develop treatments.

Recommendation Engine
Recommendation engines are data-filtering tools that make use of algorithms and data to recommend the most relevant items to a particular user.

Saama Technologies Inc.
Saama is a Silicon Valley-based company specializing in artificial intelligence-based software to automate and accelerate clinical trials for pharma companies.

Scaling
Scalability is the property of a system to handle a growing amount of work by adding resources to the system.

Sprints
A sprint is a time-boxed iteration of a continuous development cycle. Within a sprint, the planned amount of work has to be completed by the team and made ready for review. Scrum Agile methodology uses this term widely.

STEM
STEM is an acronym for the fields of science, technology, engineering, and math.

Turing Award
The Turing Award is an annual prize given by the Association for Computing Machinery (ACM) to an individual selected for contributions "of lasting and primary technical importance to the computer field."

AI Timeline

Thousands of people across the globe worked for countless hours resulting in the current-generation artificial intelligence advances that we enjoy today. The historical journey of AI is explained here through a few key events. Only critical events related to the theme of this book are mentioned here, due to the brevity of space.

1950 TURING TEST

Computer scientist Alan Turing proposed a test for machine intelligence. If a machine can trick humans into thinking it is human, then it is intelligent—that is the premise of the Turing Test.

1955 AI DEFINITION

The term "artificial intelligence" was born. Computer scientist John McCarthy defined it as "the science and engineering of making intelligent machines."

1964 ELIZA

A pioneering chatbot developed at MIT which held conversations with humans.

The 1970s to 1980s AI WINTER

The moment that historians pinpoint as the end of the AI winter was when AI's commercial value started to be realized, attracting new investment. Period of a revival of the bottom-up approach to AI, including the long-unfashionable field of neural networks.

1997 DEEP BLUE

A chess-playing computer named Deep Blue developed by IBM defeated the then-reigning world champion, Garry Kasparov.

2002 ROOMBA

IRobot Company developed the first mass-produced autonomous robotic vacuum cleaner. ROOMBA could learn and navigate its way to clean homes.

2011 WATSON

IBM's question-answering computer, Watson won first place on the popular television quiz show, *Jeopardy.*

2014 ALEXA

Amazon launched Alexa, an intelligent virtual assistant with a voice interface to complete shopping tasks.

2017 ALPHAGO

Google's AI machine, AlphaGo, beat world champion Ke Jie in the complex board game of Go, notable for its vast number (2^{170}) of possible positions.

2018 DALIA

Deep Learning Virtual Assistant, DaLIA, was released by Saama Technologies to answer the complex questions of clinical research personnel with a natural language interface.

AI Trailblazers

Details of a few trailblazers who contributed to some of the concepts mentioned in this book and beyond are highlighted below to acknowledge and respect their works. Only a select list of people is included here, due to the brevity of space.

Alan Turing (1912-1954)

Turing was an English mathematician, computer scientist, logician, philosopher, and theoretical biologist. Turing was highly influential in the development of theoretical computer science, providing a formalization of the concepts of algorithm and computation with the Turing machine, which can be considered a model of a general-purpose computer.

John McCarthy (1927-2011)

McCarthy was an American computer and cognitive scientist. McCarthy was one of the founders of the discipline of artificial intelligence. He coined the term "artificial intelligence," developed the Lisp programming language, and was very influential in the early development of AI.

Marvin Minsky (1927-2016)

Minsky was an American cognitive scientist concerned mainly with the research of artificial intelligence, the co-founder of MIT's AI laboratory, and the author of several texts relating to AI and philosophy.

Andrew Ng

Ng is a Chinese-American businessman, computer scientist, investor, and writer. As a businessman and investor, Ng co-founded and led Google Brain and was a former Vice President and Chief Scientist at Baidu.

Dabbala Rajagopal "Raj" Reddy

Dr. Raj Reddy is an Indian-American computer scientist and a winner of the Turing Award. He is one of the early pioneers of artificial intelligence and has served on the faculty of Stanford and Carnegie Mellon for over fifty years. He was the founding director of the Robotics Institute at Carnegie Mellon University and a recipient of the Padma Bhushan award from the Indian government.

Demetris Zambas

Demetris is a clinical operations leader spearheading several innovations across data management in clinical trials. His pioneering work in using Artificial Intelligence to challenge the traditional query management methods for clinical data analysis is paving the way for unprecedented efficiencies and reliability for the pharma industry. Demetris is currently the Global Head of Data Monitoring and Management at Pfizer. He serves on several Boards, including SCDM's Advisory Board.

Demis Hassabis

Hassabis is a British artificial intelligence researcher, neuroscientist, video game designer, entrepreneur, and five-times winner of the Pentamind board games championship. He is the CEO and co-founder of DeepMind.

Fei-Fei Li

Li is a Chinese-born American computer scientist, nonprofit executive, and writer. She is a professor at Stanford University and the co-director of Stanford's Human-Centered AI Institute and the Stanford Vision and Learning Lab.

Geoffrey Hinton

Hinton is an English Canadian cognitive psychologist and computer scientist, most noted for his work on artificial neural networks. Since 2013, he's divided his time between working for Google (Google Brain) and the University of Toronto.

Hilary Mason

Mason is an American data scientist and the founder of technology startup Fast Forward Labs, as well as a Data Scientist in Residence at Accel Partners.

Ian Goodfellow

Goodfellow is a researcher working in machine learning, employed at Apple as its director of machine learning in the Special Projects Group. He worked as a research scientist at Google Brain before Apple.

Jeff Dean

Dean is an American computer scientist and software engineer. He is currently the lead of Google AI, Google's AI division, and the co-designer and co-implementer of generations of Google's crawling indexing and query retrieval systems.

Ken Coleman

Ken is a member of the Executive Leadership Council and the Dean's Advisory Council for the Fisher College of Business at The Ohio State University. He mentors people in various stages of their careers and has been a passionate champion for diversity. He is a recipient of countless leadership and diversity awards and honors. Ken serves on several Boards and is a Special Advisor to both the Andreessen Horowitz Venture Capital Firm and the Carrick Capital Partners Private Equity Firm.

Kumar Vadaparty

Vadaparty is an Indian-American computer scientist and a strong proponent of the open-hardware movement, and establishing decentralized manufacturing capabilities across the world. A former university faculty and researcher at Bell Communications Research, he currently works as a Distinguished Engineer and Executive Director at Morgan Stanley.

Limor Fried

Fried is an American electrical engineer and owner of the electronics hobbyist company Adafruit Industries. She is influential in the open-source hardware community, and in the drafting of the *Open Source Hardware definition*.

Malaikannan Sankarasubbu ('Malai')

Malai is an AI researcher and developer of Deep Learning-based systems and Virtual Assistants. Expert in designing applications to help pharma companies reduce cycle time to manage and understand clinical study data. Currently, he is the head of AI Research Labs at Saama Technologies Inc.

Megan Price

Executive Director of the Human Rights Data Analysis Group, Price collects and analyses data to investigate violations of human rights. She earned a Ph.D. in biostatistics from the Rollins School of Public Health in 2009.

Mehdi Benchoufi

Mehdi is a medical doctor, mathematician involved in several international projects at the institutional level. His pioneering academic field related to Blockchain usages in clinical trials and in many international working groups in new technology in healthcare is well acclaimed. He is currently working as a Researcher in Clinical Epidemiology at Hotel Dieu Hospital, Region de Paris, France, and is on the Board of Advisors for Saama Technologies.

Michael I Jordan

Jordan is an American scientist and professor at the University of California, Berkeley, and a researcher in machine learning, statistics, and artificial intelligence. In 2016, *Science* reported him as the world's most influential computer scientist.

Richard Sutton

Sutton is an American computer scientist, currently a distinguished research scientist at DeepMind, and a professor of computing science at the University of Alberta. Sutton is considered one of the founding fathers of modern computational reinforcement learning.

Yann LeCun

LeCun is a French-American computer scientist working primarily in the fields of machine learning, computer vision, mobile robotics, and computational neuroscience. He is the Silver Professor of the Courant Institute of Mathematical Sciences at New York University, and Vice President, Chief AI Scientist at Facebook.

Yoshua Bengio

A Canadian computer scientist, Bengio is most noted for his work on artificial neural networks and deep learning. He was a co-recipient of the 2018 ACM A.M. Turing Award for his work in deep learning. He is a professor at the Department of Computer Science and Operations Research at the Université de Montréal.

Author: Sagar Anisingaraju

Based out of San Jose, California, Sagar Anisingaraju currently works as Chief Strategy Officer at Saama Technologies, USA. He was born in Visakhapatnam, India. He did his Bachelor's in Engineering at Andhra University and Master's at IIT Kanpur. After an early stint in mathematical font design systems at CMC Ltd., Sagar immigrated to the USA in 1995.

Sagar's professional passion is helping pharma and biotech companies create analytical solutions with technology and artificial intelligence to solve the business challenges around clinical trials and drug development.

Sagar's personal passions revolve around creative writing and gameplay. His innovations include the creation and conduct of word- and content-formation games in multiple languages using technology and language tools. His works are published as Game Books under the brand <u>Kokkoroko</u> and are played daily in social media groups.

Kuchela.AI is Sagar's first fictional work. It emerged out of his work experiences, beliefs, and passion that advances in artificial intelligence have a significant role to play in improving human productivity across all walks of life. He has chosen a fictional backdrop to explain the basics of artificial intelligence in the simplest of terms. Sagar is committed to helping the youth learn the concepts and advances explained in this book to build App platforms such as Kuchela.AI to create social benefits across the world.

Author: Prasad Chaganti

Based out of Hyderabad, India, Prasad Chaganti currently works as Chief Manager at State Bank of India. He was born in Amalapuram, India. He did his Master's in Commerce at Nagpur University.

Daily interactions with customers at work, their life stories, the influence of several authors, and passion for literature led Prasad to start writing his works.

His first book titled "Aa Paatha Madhuralu," a nostalgic recollection of childhood memories, was well acclaimed and published in 2017. His short stories were published and won awards in several Telugu magazines and newspapers, including Swati, Saakshi, Chandamama, Velugu, Prajasakthi, and others.

Prasad's passion for native Konaseema area where he was born and a unique storytelling capability to show human values and culture in a simple to understand Telugu language is exemplified and penned in his book 'Kona Seema Kadhalu.' His religious under pinning's, belief in Lord Shiva, and the power of the almighty were explained in several of his short stories and essays. A collection of them is being published under 'Shivaarpanam.'

Prasad co-authored with Sagar Anisingaraju for Kuchela.AI in the Telugu language, out of his firm belief that technology's real benefits are realized only when they are scaled to the underprivileged.

Made in the USA
Monee, IL
11 August 2020